A Tale of Lambiq City

This book is written by Mohammad Hamza and contains an enthusiastic story of four men who got lost on an island called Lambiq City. Read it to know When one person opens the door which he does not have to open.

Mohammad Hamza

Notion press publications

printed in 2023

NOTION PRESS

3rd Floor, 6768, Chandra Bhavan, New, Nehru Place-110019.

phone no: +91 44 46315631

email: publish@notionpress.com

website: https://notionpress.com

cover by: Mohammad Hamza

Written by: Mohammad Hamza

ISBN: 979-889133523-3

printed in India.

“A STORY OF FOUR FRIENDS”

CONTENTS

1. NICE TO MEET YOU, BRAD

Once upon a time, there lived a man in England named Ethan. He lived with his wife Marie and his two-month-old daughter.

Ethan has been interested in adventure since his childhood. When he was ten years old, he and his uncle William went on an exploration. They traveled from England to the Indian Ocean with only two crew members when a great sea monster hit their ship. Somehow, they managed to get to an island where they saw an inexpressible creature. They got scared. But they were hungry. Hunger took over the reins, and they ran after that creature to satiate their hunger.

"We need to find a way out," said one of the crewmembers.

“To survive, we need food. But how can we get it?” asked Ethan.

“Your father must be searching for us in the ocean, but we need to survive here for a few days," said William.

"Look! There is a rabbit," exclaimed one of the crew members.

"Looks like we don't have much of an option to choose our food," said William sadly.

"Let's hunt, Uncle," said Ethan.

After some time, they were able to capture the rabbit. All of them were happy with their prize. They started a bonfire to cook and keep wild animals away.

"Oh, it tastes like a lump of raw meat," said Ethan.

"Don't be cheeky," said William wryly.

"You must have come here to attain the egg," said a voice.

"Oh, who are you?" asked a crewmember.

They saw a man approach their bonfire.

"I was a trader once but lost my ship four years ago. Since then, I have been living here. And now I feel at home," said the man.

He sat with them without waiting for an invitation to join.

"A long time ago, when tigers used to smoke," started the man again," a king named Dazzle lived on this island. He had a huge army. He also loved his countrymen, but unfortunately, a person named Dragon, who wanted to destroy the whole island started disturbing the countrymen. His complaints start reaching the king.

Ethan and others were now totally grasped by the man's story.

"As you know, the king loved his people. He ordered his soldiers to bring him to his court where he would hang him." the man went on. "Finally, the soldiers caught him. He was presented in the court, where the king ordered him to be hanged. Days passed and then the day came by when the Dragon was supposed to be hanged. Before hanging him, the king asked him for his last word. Then the Dragon cursed the king, a real dragon would kill him. The king did not believe him then."

"A few days later, the king announced his princess's marriage to the most beautiful boy in the country. For some medical reason, the prince died, and the princess got very ill. No medicine could cure the princess, and the princess died. Many new diseases started spreading, and the day came when a huge dragon attacked the kingdom. The army was huge, so they managed to kill the dragon, but the main motive of the dragon was to kill the king, which it did!" the man exclaimed.

"The king died." The man ended his story.

"Oh, what a story, said Ethan.

"It's not a story. It's real." said the man.

“Ah, you were talking about the egg,” William remembered.

"I think so. Yes, a huge construction was going on in the kingdom, and they found the egg of the dragon.” said the man.

“But how do you know all about this?" asked Ethan.

“I know this because the queen had mentioned this to me. She died three years ago," said the man.

“Oh! So, sad.” said one of the crewmembers.

“I don’t believe this man. Where is the egg now?” asked Ethan.

"It’s down the country. The country is abandoned now.” said the trader.

“Take us to the egg, please,” requested William.

“Why? No, never,” said Ethan.

“Just do as I said,” said William, ignoring Ethan.

They all walked through the forest and reached the country, where they saw an orange-colored egg. They searched for anything special they could find when, suddenly, the dragon egg started to hatch. Everybody got scared, and the small dragon came out of it. The mother dragon emerged out of nowhere and leaped towards Ethan to attack him. But William saved him, and the dragon hit William. The crew members took Ethan and started running away, and they saw the ship of Ethan’s father, which came to their rescue. Ethan's father sailed them home. The crew members told the whole story.

One fine morning, Ethan was browsing through the newspaper headlines when he found an article about Lambic City. The newspaper article mentioned prize money for the Lambic City explorers. He got excited.

He contacted that person and came to know his name was Brad.

****

Brad was an explorer himself and used to go on adventures now and then. Like Ethan, he also had some ghosts lurking in his past. His father passed away during a sea voyage. When he was just nine, he was playing in the snow. He was having fun. While he was skating, Brad fell from the mountain and got dwelled. Her mom and father searched for him but couldn't find him.

A few days later, a boy who was building a snowman found Brad. Brad was still alive in the snow for the last 14-15 days. This showed that he has some connection with snow.

Ethan told him that he wanted to go to Lambiq City. This magical city was close to South Africa. Brad told him that he would require permission from the government and then only he could ready the ship. He also informed Ethan that the total expenses would be around 7000 pounds.

Ethan somehow managed to contact the government and got permission by signing the declaration in case he died while discovering Lambiq City.

The contract which he signed with the government was as follows-

"I, Ethan, son of Jacob Hunt, declare and accept to go on the journey of discovering the unknown City of Lambiq with my own free will. The voyage is going to start on 17th May 1912.

I am aware of the dangers of this journey and accept the known reward set by the government, which is 1000,000 pounds for a complete exploration of the city. Whatever I get there will belong to the government.

In case of my death during this voyage under any circumstances, my family has a right to claim 7,000 pounds from the government treasury."

After signing the declaration, he showed them to Brad and started to prepare for their upcoming journey. The government provided them with powerful weapons like guns and katanas.

A Katana is a weapon made of a unique metal available only in the country of England called chromium. It can easily cut through a tree without a dent on its blade.

The bullets were also optimized to make them strong enough to pierce any metal they were shot on.

While preparing for the oncoming journey, both Ethan and Brad became good friends. Two more men were going with them: John and James. They named the ship **Rt Voyage**.

Both James and John were adventurous by nature. To everyone's surprise, they looked very much alike. This was a mystery for both John and James.

James was born after his father's death. James's mother had also adopted a boy named John, who was of the same age as James. Both James and John weren't aware that John had been adopted.

When they were 16 years old, James' mother finally thought about disclosing the secret to her son, James. One day, she found James on their balcony all alone. She approached him and told him the whole story of how she found John in the streets of Milton. She also requested James not to disclose this secret to John.

She never knew that she poured her heart out in front of John instead of James! She couldn't realize who was standing on the balcony in front of her. John never mentioned this tragic confusion to her as well.

All 4 comrades were ready to ride to their death.

2. A WAY TO THE LAMBIQ CITY

On 17th May 1912, Ethan and his friends set sail towards Lambiq city, thus commencing their adventure. Brad told Ethan that he had planned a party, and Ethan agreed with it. They started the party on the ship's deck at night, and the crew sang and danced to the beats of James's whistle.

After getting tired from dancing, they started having their meal with sleepy wine. Brad offered it to Ethan, but Ethan had stopped drinking wine 2 years back. After further inquiry, Ethan sat and started telling the story of when motor cars were new to England. One fine day Ethan's friend brought his car to Ethan to visit a wedding party together. While returning from the party, his friend was heavily drunk and couldn't keep his eyes open.

Suddenly, Ethan's eyes opened, he saw his friend lying on the sidewalk taking his last breath, and then boom, blast, and they were engulfed in flames.

The final word from Ethan's friend's mouth was, "Promise me, Ethan, you will never drink." Drinking kills. Ethan's friend's last breath warned Ethan not to drink again.

Back on the ship, everybody became emotional.

"I also have an emotional story connected to me," said Brad.

"What is that?" asked James.

"It was a few years ago. One of my best friends had a habit of smuggling and when I caught him, he told me to do the same thing and he passed me some drugs to smell. I thought of my parents and then I smelled it and it relaxed me. " After speaking this much Brad stopped.

And then he continued, "I started it daily. But then a friend came into my life and he stopped me from taking these drugs. He also warned me to stay away from those friends. I just ignored him because he was my new friend, but a time came that changed my whole life. My old friend had some connections with some more bad boys and I went to him and asked for more drugs. He gave me a pouch of drugs."

"They were not so friendly to me. They started cracking jokes on my mother and father. I couldn't tolerate it and he hit one of his new friends. The Boys got angry and they started hitting me. They left me half dead." Brad paused.

"It was then that I remembered my good friend." With this Brad ended his story.

With tears in their eyes, they helped each other to bed.

"Ethan, Wake up! Wake up!" Brad shouted.

Ethan woke up and washed his face; when he came out, Brad said, "We would be in Lambiq City in a few days."

They had their breakfast.

James shouted “Look! Look!”

“What's that”? asked Ethan.

“It is a gigantic whale. This is the whale guardian of Lambiq city,” explained Brad.

“We are near the shore of Lambiq City. I will let us in.” Brad said.

“Let's end this thing,” said Ethan.

Ethan was already prepared. He jumped into the water and tried to kill the whale with his Katana. The whale started bleeding in just two slashes but did not die. Ethan jumped onto the ship.

“The whale disappeared,” said Brad, confused.

“Where did it go?" asked James.

And then suddenly 4 whales surrounded the ship and then a whale said, “You have come to the wrong place. I gave you one chance to go back or you will suffer a painful death.”

“We just wanted to explore the city of power, Lambiq City,” said James.

“You can't, it's full of danger and I am the guardian of Lambiq city,” said the whale.

“They won’t agree to your terms,” said Ethan.

They started to hunt the whales but the whales couldn’t attack the boys because they were standing on the whales and the whales suffered a lot of attacks from Katana and then they lost hope finally.

A few days went by without any incidents.

A large sound struck Ethan's eardrum. On 2nd August, Ethan saw a pirate ship coming towards their vessel. Ethan called everyone and commanded them to be prepared.

“We have mighty swords and lethal guns. I will blast their ships”, John said.

‘But why wait? We have shurikens” exclaimed Brad. “John and James are masters in throwing it,” added Brad.

“This thing must be like becoming ninjas, it's really fun using them,” said Ethan.

"Let the ship come near us and then we will attack them with our ninja technique jumps!” said Brad.

“Ah! No!" said Ethan.

Kach…kach shuriken hits.

“Ah, nice Brad, good shot!" said John.

“But where is Ethan?” asked James.

“I am here, " said Ethan. "Help me to get out of this place."

After taking out Ethan they went to take a rest.

”We are going to rest for a while,” said Brad.

The following day, when the ship approached closer to the island, Brad discovered a colossal tree thrice the size of a regular one.

“Oh, I think it is Lambiq City”, Brad said

“Let us rob all the powers of this city,” said Ethan.

3. DISCOVERY OF THE NEW PLACE

They reached the shore. They started finding wood and charcoal. They made a wooden shelter.

“Hey, what's that”? James asked

“No, something dangerous again”, John cried.

“It's looking like a witch's house,” Ethan said.

"Yeah, it's the house of a witch!" A lady said.

“Hey Brad, why are you changing your voice,” John said.

“I am not changing,’ Brad said.

“So who's that? Ah...ah... a witch,” John cried.

“Hey, who are you?” Brad asked.

“Don't be afraid. I believe you must have come here to attain powers." the witch said.

“Hell.... yeah!” Ethan replied excitedly.

“I will help you to defeat all bosses because I want to help this cursed land to be set free. Go take some rest for today because tomorrow you have to work hard. Hurry now.” said the witch.

The Friends returned to their shelter and had their meal.

“Bolt the main door”, Brad said.

The next morning, Ethan was the last to wake up, and he came out of the house where he saw the witch.

“What's your name”? Ethan asked.

“What will you do with my name”? The old lady asked.

(Brad, John, and James came out of the cottage).

“My name is Hallie”, the witch said.

“What??” James exclaimed. “It is our mother's name but…” James stopped.

“But what?” Ethan asked.

“But she died," John cried.

“What happened to your mother”? Hallie asked.

“My father served in the army and died at the borders of England. My mother couldn't believe it, and she died in the evening on a dreadful, stormy night. We couldn't save her.” James stopped.

"My name is Hallie." Hallie started telling them about herself; “I lived here with my parents. My mother was a very kind woman, and my father had a dream to become the water boss. He successfully defeated the water boss and took all his powers for himself. I have never heard of him from that day, nor has he come back".

"My name is Brad, and my father was the captain of two ships." Brad stopped and took a long breath, then continued, "But on 19th May 1846, it was reported by the navy that he and his ships drowned along with his 17 crewmates. I have only my mother and my father's other ship left in this world" answered Brad.

Ethan was the last to tell his story. *Now it's my turn* Ethan was thinking.

"My father and mother are dead. I lost them in a train accident" Ethan stopped.

"Tell us what happened", John said.

"I was just 17 years old at that time; We boarded the train for Liverpool, it was a night journey, and the train tracks were still in construction. Due to some issues, the train's light was not working well. The driver couldn't see the sign of the workers. In between the lights flickering, he rushed the train into a dam, there was no water in the dam, and the train fell from 25 to 30 meters. There were huge casualties. Many people died, and the government announced a gift of 10000 pounds for any survivor relative of this accident. In a week, I received 20000 pounds from the government. Days passed, and I tried to overcome the sadness when I met a girl named Marie and decided to marry her. I now have a small daughter, Rose, who is waiting for his father's return", ended Ethan.

"It's noon, go and eat lunch," the old lady said.

"But... I have a question: who are the other bosses?" asked Brad.

"I will tell you later", the old lady said.

After eating lunch, they went to Hallie's house.

They sat at the dining table; Hallie arrived at the dining table and told them about four bosses.

Hallie started explaining "There are four bosses

Air boss

Water boss

Earth boss

Fire boss

The air boss is the weakest of them all. The water boss is my father as I had mentioned earlier. I will try to convince him. Earth's boss is also powerful. The fire boss is the strongest of all the bosses".

The witch continued, "Now, if you think we only have to defeat the bosses, then you are wrong; every boss has his palace and bodyguards. Every bodyguard has his power. The air bodyguards are invisible, hence we can't see them. We can only see them by drinking the invisible potion."

"Water bodyguards can breathe underwater, earth bodyguards are made of stones, and fire bodyguards are fire resistant." Hallie finished.

"Tomorrow be prepared, we have to go somewhere", said Hallie again.

They went to sleep.

4. MEETING WITH THE POWERS

The following day, Ethan was the last to leave his bed. He rushes to Hallie's house; he encounters two cows with a mushroom on their head, pulling a cart where his friends are sitting. He joined them, reaching a mysterious place in a few hours.

Hallie started by saying “There are five stones, one in the middle and the four stones covering it. When you kill all the bosses, you have to cut the head of the bosses and put on those four stones covering the middle stone. After you keep all the heads, four bosses, and four stones, the center stone will own the power right now”, Hallie said.

"Let's see all the bosses and his palace," said Hallie and started reading magical words. This is the palace of the air boss,’ Hallie said.

“Come back”, Hallie shouted;

“Let's now go to the water boss," Brad said.

“Yes, but we must come fast because the water boss palace is underwater, so we can't breathe,” said Hallie.

“Oh, I can't breathe," John muttered.

They didn't wait a single second to come back!

"No! The earth boss has his palace in plain land, no sign of trees we can't breathe." John said. The same thing happened. They came back.

“Let us go to Fire Boss palace,” James said.

“We can't go. We have not drunk the fire resistance potion, and we can die there” said Hallie.

“So let's prepare to kill the Air boss,” said John.

“But, wait,” said Hallie.

“Why”? Asked Ethan

“There is something I want to tell you” Hallie started. "There once lived one of the most powerful kings named Nadara. He was very powerful in Lambiq city. He was very cruel. He chose some of his officials to help him protect himself from any danger. And in return, he promised to keep them safe. But they didn’t help Nadara, instead, they dethroned him. Nadara couldn't kill the officials because he had promised not to hurt them and to protect them from any danger. Unfortunately, he had to keep his promise.”

“Oh," said Brad.

After listening to the long speech of Hallie. “But why is it connected to these bosses?” asked Ethan.

“Yes! These officials are the bosses, after becoming very powerful these four bosses separate themselves and become too strong” said Hallie.

“That means that those four officials have become the bosses,” said James.

“Yes,” replied Hallie.

“So how good is that Nadara?” asked Brad.

“He is very strong and nearly impossible to kill but only when he has his swords, if not then he is useless” answered Hallie.

“So how will take his sword” asked James,

“It’s very easy, we just need to blow up his swords room,” answered Hallie.

“How can we blow up his room?” asked John,

“We need gunpowder and sand spears,” said Hallie.

“What is a sand spear?” asked John,

“It is used to light up gunpowder,” replied Hallie.

“So I knew the place from where to get it,” Hallie said.

“But why kill Nadara?" asked James.

Everybody ignored him.

"So let's prepare to kill him," everyone said.

5. END OF NADARA

The next morning, Hallie visited the shelter of Ethan, Brad, John, and James. She told them that gunpowder is very easy to get and they can get it in the caves of Jonk because there are some creatures who when killed, their body gives out gunpowder."

"So when we were going to collect?" asked James.

"Right now," said Ethan.

They moved on in search of the cave. After a few blocks of moving, they saw a large cave with some monsters inside it when James went near them the monsters blasted!

"What is that"? Asked John randomly.

James got injured.

"Don't go near it or the monsters will blast" Ethan killed a monster by throwing a shuriken at the monsters.

After that, all of them started to use their shuriken. Then they collected some of the gunpowder and returned. After that, they returned to their home and rested for a while, and then Hallie came to their house.

"The sand spear could only be got by a group of people named the Jodar group. This is a tribal group but they are very aggressive so be careful. But before that, you must learn their language," said Hallie.

"So who is going to learn the language?" asked Ethan.

Everybody started looking at Ethan.

"Ah! No" cried Ethan.

Some of the important words Ethan needs to learn are sand spear, help, bosses, and many other things. After learning the language for three to five days, Ethan and his friends went to that tribal group when they reached there the tribal group took them to their king, the king asked in his language what Ethan wanted,

Ethan told them, "I want a sand spear."

After listening to Ethan the tribal king said, "I will only help you if you help us to kill a monster who has been trying to attack the tribal group."

Ethan agreed with his terms and went to his shelter. "So, we need to keep only Katana?" asked James.

"Yes, only Katana," replied Brad.

When they again reached the tribal group, some of the Jodar group people took Ethan to the place where the monster was enjoying his sleep. The sword attacked the neck of the monster and the monster cried in pain and started to breathe his last air. After killing the monster, the

Jodar group kept their promise. They provided Ethan with some sand spears and after taking all the sand spears Ethan went to his shelter. After that, they rest for a day and the day comes to defeat the Nadara. Hallie took her mushroom cow and they rode to the Nadara base. When they reached the most dangerous base they saw Nadara sitting in front of the base.

"How can we go there"? asked John.

"Wait a bit," said James.

After moving a bit further, they slowly reached the base but Nadara was in his base so they couldn't blow up the base.

"What do we need to do?" asked Ethan.

"We need to wait for the correct time," said Hallie.

After some time, Nadara was out of the base and moved in another direction. Then they started to place gunpowder all around. While Brad was placing the gunpowder, Nadara saw him and he started following him. It was too late.

"Lit up the base!" shouted John.

And the base was in dust. Nadara now didn't have any sword in his hand and Ethan started attacking Nadara. After some attacks, Ethan, Brad, John, and James paused and returned. They thought that Nadara had died, but that wasn't the case.

After reaching the house, they were very excited after their first winning

“Ah, where can we find the invisible potion to kill Air boss?” John asked enthusiastically.

“I will tell you later,” replied Hallie.

After the celebration, it was time for the heroes to sleep but their adrenaline got in their way.

Why sleep when they have their biggest comedian, John, to crack some funny jokes and tell us some horror or scary stories that will make Ethan pee in his pants? After some crack jokes and horror stories they finally went to their shelter to sleep. After a small dream, Brad heard the voice of Ethan shouting. Brad woke up and he saw Nadara standing in front of Brad.

“How is it possible”? asked Brad.

Then Nadara was going to attack Brad, he stood up and saved himself from Nadara's attack and Nadara looked very angry.

“We have to steal the sword of Nadara but how?” asked John.

“Like this,” said Ethan and jumped onto the face of Nadara and filled the sand in his eyes.

“Oh I can’t see,” said Nadara,

“Take his sword,” said Ethan

Brad, John, and James started to pull the sword from his hand of Nadara but Nadara was strong. Ethan jumped on the hand of Nadara.

“Ahh!” Cried Nadara.

Ethan took his sword and threw it took out his mightiest katana and attacked Nadara. Now Nadara was not breathing and this was their first victory.

6. AN ATTEMPT TO DEFEAT THE AIR BOSS

The next day, they started preparing for battle.

"We need high water, which is very useful", Hallie said.

"Why?" John asked.

"When you are invisible, and the other person is Invisible too. But, if you consume high water, then the other person cannot see you, but you can see him" replied Hallie.

"Where will we get it"? Ethan asked.

"High water is found in the stomachs of 3-headed sharks," Hallie replied.

"3 headed sharks?" Brad asked.

"Yes", replied Hallie.

"Okay, let us move to kill 3-headed sharks", James said.

They went to the seashore.

By swords, the main thing is the target of my life, Ethan thought.

"Yeah", Ethan shouted.

He cut one head off the shark, and the shark is no more.

Ethan asked. “Why kill only one head, they all die”?

“It's too milky," said James.

“Listen”, said Hallie “if we drink the high water, we can be invisible for only 3 min. To increase the time we want a particular type of lily ball that is very useful. It increases the time by 5 minutes. It grows in the mountains.”

“I have the map. Tomorrow, you can go," said Hallie.

Everyone went to sleep but the worm inside the brain of Ethan was not feeling sleepy. He stole the map from Hallie's house and started following it.

It took a few minutes to reach the place. He reached the mountain and climbed the hill. White lily ball shins in front of Ethan, but he can't take

“What”? Ethan muttered.

Ethan saw a wolf-like creature just in front of the lily ball, the beast saw Ethan, and howled; many wolves came out. Ethan steps back; *Oh shit, no land.*

Ethan falls from the mountain, but he survives. He runs towards his cottage, but his eyes are closed in the middle of the way.

The next morning. “Hey! Brad! Forget to tell you that on the way to finding Lily, you will see many creatures called howlers.” Hallie said.

"Can't you tell this before?” Ethan said.

“Oh my God, what happened to you, Ethan?" Hallie asked.

Ethan told the whole story. Everyone makes fun of them.

“Now let's go to find the lily ball,” said Brad.

They reached the place.

They killed all the monsters and collected the lily ball, but suddenly a creature jumped on Brad and bit his hand. They came back.

“I have one thing that will save you from the poisoned creature”, said Hallie.

“Ah”, Brad muttered in pain.

Hallie heated the knife and burned Brad's hand. Brad screamed.

The following day everyone was ready with their equipment; they called the two cows and sat on them.

In a few hours, they reached the place.

Hallie opened the gate of the air boss dimension, and everybody got inside. She made the invisible potion and added high water and lily balls to it; everybody drank the elixir.

“Sit, kill the two bodyguards at the gate with your gun,” said Hallie.

John and James killed the two bodyguards at the entrance, and they entered the palace slowly.

“There they are,” John said.

“No, don't mess with the army, find the air boss room, he is prominent,” said Hallie.

After walking for two to three minutes, they saw a big gate.

They went inside it, and their potion time ended.

“I don't know who you are, but I know why you came here”, said the air boss.

“Attack!" shouted the Air boss.

Many monsters came out (they started fighting), and a vast sword hit the neck of the beast. Ethan, John, and James cut the two monsters in two halves Brad hit the stomach of the beast.

They saw green liquid coming out of the monster.

"Ah, nice, you kill all the monsters," said the air boss.

John and James loaded the gun and shot at the air boss, but the air boss lifted John in the air and threw him to the wall; this was the moment Ethan and Brad were waiting for. When the air boss kneeled, they both attacked the neck of the air boss and the head came out of his body; the air boss was no more, but John was severely injured.

They keep the head of the air boss in the bag.

And started moving backward, there were many invisible potions in the air boss room they drank them and moved out of the palace and dimension.

They reached their home.

They treated John and went to sleep.

7. AN ATTEMPT TO DEFEAT THE WATER BOSS

“Hey, we need something new,” said Hallie.

“What”? asked James.

“Does anybody remember the green liquid coming out of the monster? That is very useful. We can breathe underwater by drinking it." said Hallie.

“Excellent, we have lily balls; we can quickly increase the time,” said John.

“Yes," replied Hallie.

“The monster can be found in the deep valley of Jessica,” said Hallie.

"We will do it tomorrow," said Brad.

Everyone agrees with it.

Ethan's mind was rolling. Last time he could not bring the lily on his own, so he decided to get the green liquid on his own. This time, he needed to be strong so nobody could make fun of him anymore. He went to Hallie's house and searched for the map. He couldn't find the map, so he went on his own. After walking, he reached a valley. *This must be the valley of Jessica,* Ethan thought.

He went further. He saw two people searching for something.

“Oh, it's you, John and James!" Ethan said.

“We are here to find the green liquid,” said James.

“Me too,” said Ethan, avoiding eye contact.

“Do you have the map?” asked Ethan.

“No, we searched for the map in Hallie's place but couldn't find it,” said James.

“This means someone else had taken the map. Let's find the monster,” said Ethan.

They found a cave on the way ahead. There was a silhouette of a man in front of the cave staring at something looking confused.

“Oh! Brad?”Ethan said to James.

“We all are here in search of green liquid and the monster," said James.

“The map is showing this way”, said Brad.

They went inside the cave and started fighting with the monsters. Brad hit the eyes of the beast, John and James cut the legs of the monster, and Ethan cut the beast's stomach. They collected the liquid and came back.

The following day, they told the story to Hallie. Now they were ready, they went to the place and drank the potion of water, breathed the lily ball, and entered the water boss dimension.

Ethan killed the two bodyguards at the gate and slowly entered the palace, but the other two bodyguards saw them. Ethan cut the head of the bodyguards and drank the invisibility potion. They didn't mess with any further bodyguards. They started their search for the room of the water boss.

After eight minutes of searching, they couldn't find the room. Also, their invisibility of the potion ended. They saw two bodyguards entering a corridor; they started following them and reached the water boss's room.

They were now in the water.

“How would we fight with the water boss?" asked James.

“'We can,” replied Ethan.

“Who are you?" said the bodyguard and started to attack Ethan.

Ethan hits the sword and divides the monster into two halves.

“Huh! You all will die," the water boss said.

“Yeah?” Ethan tried to attack the water boss.

But he couldn't get near the water boss because of the water's high pressure and waves.

“You can't come near me,” the water boss boasted.

They couldn't go near the water boss, and they were tired too. The water boss was powerful under the water. They used guns, but that also failed.

Suddenly, Hallie remembers one thing...

She slowly started speaking some magical words, and she started coming near the water boss. The water boss was shocked. Then he remembered that he had taught these powers to only one person in the world. It didn't even take him a second to realize that she was his daughter. The water boss hugged Hallie.

“Father, these are my friends,” said Hallie.

The waves stopped. “Father, can you give us your powers to one of my friends?" asked Hallie.

“Yes, I am getting old”, said the water boss.

They came back from the water boss dimension.

The water boss was ready to help Ethan.

They made a big and giant house for the water boss, but how can the water boss survive on land by powers, or is there any secret?

8. AN ATTEMPT TO DEFEAT EARTH BOSS

“So now, everybody listens carefully about the Earth boss' palace. There will be no mountains, no hills, and not even trees. It would be plain”, said Hallie. "So as you know, we can't breathe without trees. So I have collected some green liquid from the monsters. This green liquid will help us breathe without oxygen. Let's rest for a while, and then we will go to take the head of Earth boss.”

After resting for a few minutes, they started preparing for the next dimension.

“Let us go. There is no time," said Ethan.

They reached the place with the help of the Water boss. They went inside the dimension.

“Hey, this is strange. Earth boss has no bodyguards at the gate,” said Hallie.

“They are over there”, John said, pointing upwards.

John started shooting them with arrows. Ethan and John killed them, and they slowly tried to open the gate, but the gate was closed from inside.

“How will we go”? asked James.

"There are some secret gates over here; let's find out," said Ethan.

"No, it will be a waste of time. I will take you all to the terrace and find a way down." the Water boss said to Brad.

They landed on the terrace and started finding a way down to the room.

"Wait! Drink this invisible potion," said Hallie.

"I will make a hole so that we can go down. The monsters are in the staircase." said the Water boss.

"But if someone hears the sound of digging? Ethan asked.

"We are invisible." John corrected.

The palace stone broke with the water pressure, and they got down slowly. They saw many soldiers coming towards them. As they were invisible no bodyguards could find them.

"What do we do now? They are searching for us!" asked John.

"We can do only one thing to divert their mind from us," Hallie pointed out.

"I have an idea," James explained. "Water boss will make one more hole like that, and all four of us will leave from here."

“Excellent idea,” said Hallie.

The water boss moved to another place and started digging. The stone broke and fell. Everybody rushed to that place and looked at what had happened.

The four adventurers rushed out of the room and started finding the room of the Earth boss.

They kept on searching for the Earth boss's room. After some time, the Water boss also joined their search. They slowly opened the gate and to their surprise! They couldn't find anyone in that room. They started searching for the Earth boss all over the room.

“There must be some secret way, " said the Water boss.

“I agree," said Brad.

“Hey, look here, the wall is a bit different,” said John, breaking one of the walls.

“No, the soldiers will come here, find a lever or button, " said Ethan.

After searching for some time, they finally found the lever.

Ethan pressed the lever, and suddenly the gate opened; they entered the corridor and rushed towards the aisle to the room. They slowly opened the gate and saw the Earth boss.

“Hey, who are you?” asked the Earth boss.

“How did you get in?" asked the Earth boss again.

“I am your departure,” said Ethan.

“Oh, let's see,” said the Earth boss.

The Earth boss reached out for Brad and threw him towards the nearby wall. John started to shoot at him, and Ethan cut his leg. The Earth boss couldn't tolerate the pressure of the Water boss. And the Earth boss lay down; he was significantly injured. Still, he lifted Hallie, threw her on the Water boss, and then captured both of them. But Ethan attacked the Earth boss on his neck, and the Earth boss died; they slowly moved back from the Earth boss's palace. Brad and Hallie were severely injured. They needed something to treat them so Ethan followed the medicine-making step told by the Water boss.

9. AN ATTEMPT TO DEFEAT FIRE BOSS

“We are not ready because the Fire boss is the strongest of all the bosses, and we have to make an exceptional fire resistance,” said Hallie. "It's just the same as the lily ball, but it has fire on it."

“So we can easily recognize it,” said Ethan.

“So it's easy, but at night only we can get it,” said Ethan again.

"So let's go this evening," said Brad.

All of them agreed.

“Water boss can quickly bring the lily ball,” James said.

" I will also go,” said John.

“Okay you can also go,” said Ethan.

“Let's go!” John and the Water boss said in chorus.

They reached the place and John collected the lily balls.

“This was easy,” said John.

But suddenly fire howlers came out to attack. John cut the head of the howlers but by that time, one howler bit the

Water boss's leg. Then John cut the howler's leg. The Water boss crushed one of the howlers with his leg, and they came back from the place.

“So tomorrow we will go to the fire boss dimension,” said Hallie.

“So we will not waste time and get up early”, said James.

The next morning, everyone got up early and started preparing to defeat the Fire boss.

“Is everyone ready?” asked James.

“Yes, I just have to keep the potions,” said John, keeping the brews in his bag.

“Now, let's move”, said Hallie.

They reached the place where they entered the dimension and saw many bodyguards. They shot the bodyguards with an assault rifle. After killing the bodyguards they slowly moved towards the gate and tried to open it. But it was closed. They slowly drank a fire resistance potion and kept an invisible potion in the bag.

They found a rope hanging from the palace's terrace. They were climbing the rope when John's bag fell, and all the potions in the bag broke.

“Oh No, the load has fallen”, said John.

"Okay, don't get demotivated. We can fight the bodyguards on our own," replied Brad.

They went up to the terrace. Many bodyguards were there. They shot the bodyguards with their arrows. Still, many bodyguards saw them and ran towards them.

"Go! I and Brad will handle them. Find the Fire boss's room." said Ethan.

Ethan cut the bodyguards in two halves. Brad attacked three bodyguards at once and started to search for the room. They found the fire boss's room, but so many bodyguards were there. They started to fight with them. Ethan cut the legs of the bodyguard, and Brad removed the head from the bodyguard's body. John and James hit the stomach of the bodyguard. The water boss hit the bodyguards with his water pressure powers.

They entered the room of the Fire boss.

"Oh, who are you? I know I have to kill you to save my powers", said the Fire boss.

The water boss moved his water pressure to the Fire boss. Brad attacked the neck, but the Fire boss threw Brad up in the air. John and James started shooting toward the Fire boss continuously. Ethan tried to hit the stomach, but the Fire boss attacked Ethan with his powers, and the Fire boss attacked his best forces towards the Water boss, and the Water boss fell hard but, The Fire boss did not lie down. Then John and James shot the bullet into the eyes of the

Fire boss. He was stuck for a second, and that was the queue for Ethan to pick up his sword and attack the Fire boss. The fire boss is now dead, but the Water boss is no more with us.

"Father!!" Hallie cried.

They cut the heads of both the bosses and while escaping from the bodyguards, they returned to their dimension. The journey has ended.

Tomorrow is the day when Ethan gets the powers, and they will move to England.

10. A WAY BACK TO ENGLAND

"Now it's time to get the powers," Ethan said to Hallie. They rushed towards the stones. Ethan took all the heads of the bosses and kept them on the stones. The middle stone came up from the ground, and the blue rays entered his forehead. Ethan got the powers they prepared for England in a few minutes with the help of Ethan's powers.

They reached the place and got the abilities and money with him. Ethan learned one thing: adventure is not the thing that you explore the world, but the adventure is that you enjoy the world.

***

www.ingramcontent.com/pod-product-compliance
Lightning Source LLC
LaVergne TN
LVHW041255150826
845673LV00008B/2602